Ready, Steady, RACE!

Smriti Prasadam-Halls & Ed Eaves

Welcome, welcome, champion racers,
MIGHTY motors,
SPEEDY chasers.

Here's the track to test your skill,
Stay the course and feel the thrill!
Ignitions on and turbos **WHIRRING**,
Pistons pumping, engines purring.

Who is going to take first place?
Ready, steady... **RACE! RACE! RACE!**

RACE CAR RANI takes the lead,
Burning rubber
with her speed.

VROOM, **VROOM, VROOMING,**
ZOOM, **ZOOM, ZOOMING!**

Stylish, sleek, she races past,
Ready, steady... *FAST! FAST! FAST!*

Here comes speedy **JONAS JET**,
He's the fastest racer yet!

SWOOPING,

SOARING,

engine roaring,

Gaining speed
up in the sky,
Ready, steady...

FLY, FLY, FLY!

TRINI TRAIN
is right on track,
She hurtles on, not looking back.

CHUGGING, PEEPING, WHISTLING, SCREECHING,

Swift and smooth,
she's racing through,
Ready, steady...
CHOO, CHOO, CHOO!

The track's all bumpy, wet and steep,
Now first in line zooms **JOSHI JEEP**.

SLISHING,
SLOSHING,

SQUELCHING, SQUASHING,

He has tyres that never slip,
Ready, steady... **GRIP! GRIP! GRIP!**

SPEEDBOAT SAM gives one big swoosh,
And cuts the water with a whoosh!

SKIMMING,

SLIDING,

CHOPPING,

GLIDING,

With a splash he speeds away,
Ready, steady...

But now a super speedy stunt,
Puts **MOTORBIKE MIKE** way out in front.

Zig-zag **CURVING,**

turning, SWERVING,

The fastest motorbike there is,
Ready, steady... WHIZZ! WHIZZ! WHIZZ!

But suddenly his motor's choking,
The engine's hot and now it's **SMOKING!**

JUD-JUD-**JUDDERING,**
GASPING,
SPLUTTERING,

He'll **NEVER**
win the contest now,
He's sure he'll have to stop, but...

...WOW!

GO MIKE!

The other racers start to brake,

No one tries to overtake.

The racers want to HELP their friend,

So he can make it to the end.

Come on, Mike, just hang on in!

Well done, racers, you were GREAT!
Well done, racers, **CELEBRATE!**

Collect your trophies!
Rest! And **then** . . .

...Let's
READY, STEADY, RACE
AGAIN!